D1151316

# The Five Hundred

EILÍS DILLON was born in Galway in 1920 and died in Dublin in 1994. Her award-winning books for children and adults are internationally renowned.

*The Five Hundred* was the
WINNER OF THE IRISH CHILDREN'S BOOK TRUST
BISTO AWARD 1991

Other Eilís Dillon books from
The O'Brien Press
*The Lost Island*
*The Cruise of the Santa Maria*
*Living in Imperial Rome*
*The House on the Shore*

**Also by the Same Author**
*The Island of Ghosts*
*The Seekers*
*Down in the World*
*The Shadow of Vesuvius*
*A Herd of Deer*
*The Seals*
*The Sea Wall*
*The Singing Cave*
*The Island of Horses*
*A Family of Foxes*

# THE
# FIVE HUNDRED

## EILÍS DILLON

Illustrated by Gareth Floyd

THE O'BRIEN PRESS
DUBLIN

1011. 939/SF1

First paperback edition published 1991 by The O'Brien Press Ltd.,
20 Victoria Road, Dublin 6, Ireland.
Tel: +353 1 4923333; Fax: +353 1 4922777
E-mail books@obrien.ie
Website www.obrien.ie
Reprinted 2000.
First published in hardback 1972
by Hamish Hamilton Ltd., London.

ISBN 0-86278-262-7

Copyright for text © Eilís Dillon
Copyright for illustrations © Gareth Floyd
Copyright for typesetting, layout, editing and design
© The O'Brien Press Ltd.

All rights reserved. No part of this book may be reproduced or utilised
in any way or by any means, electronic or mechanical, including
photocopying, recording or by any information storage and retrieval
system without permission in writing from the publisher.

British Library Cataloguing-in-Publication Data
Dillon, Eilis, 1920 -
The five hundred.
I. Title II. Floyd, Gareth
823.9'14[J]

2 3 4 5 6 7 8 9 10
00 01 02 03 04 05 06

The O'Brien Press receives
assistance from

**The Arts Council**
An Chomhairle Ealaíon

Editing, layout, typesetting and design: The O'Brien Press Ltd.
Separations: C&A Print Services Ltd.
Printing: Cox & Wyman Ltd.

AS far back as he could remember, Pierino had heard Luca, his father, speak of the day when they would own a car. It need not be a big one—there was no need to cut a dash or put on airs. A Fiat Five Hundred would be the best. It was the cheapest to buy and the cheapest to mend, and the tax was half nothing. You could lift out all the seats, except the driver's seat of course, and carry almost anything in it. For taking things to the Sunday market it would be a joy and a blessing. With it, who knows what they would be able to sell, in time? Small tables and chairs would fit, and Pierino had often seen light wardrobes tied on top of such cars.

Usually when they talked about the car it was late evening and Luca was tired. He was specially tired of his present car, which was not

a car at all but only a glorified motor-scooter.
It had a square-shaped truck attached, as hot
as a frying-pan in summer and open to the
wind and the rain in winter.

"And who would take a trip to Frascati on a thing like that, or go to the sea on a warm day in summer?" Luca demanded. "It's all right for the market but I can't ask your mother, a respectable mother of a family, to lower herself by going to the beach in such a contraption."

Pierino agreed that it would not do for his mother though he liked it well enough himself. Sitting on the narrow balcony with his father in the evenings, he could see the scooter in the street below. It was very battered and rusty but Luca would not paint it again, not while he was saving for the Five Hundred. It would be sinful to spend good money on paint, that could be used for the new car.

The car would not be new, of course. There was no question of that. Amleto, another trader who had a big stand of furniture in the market, three times the size of Luca's, had promised to keep him an old Fiat until he had the money saved up. Amleto was always generous. He helped Luca to buy up small things he did not want himself, to sell at his stall, and he sometimes even sent him customers.

"Don't hurry about the car," he said. "I don't mind waiting. The children must eat. Take your time."

He was a huge waddling man whose clothes and even his hat always seemed too small for him, and he had a big heart too.

At last the day came, a hot Wednesday in May, when Luca dropped the last five-thousand-lire note into the box of car-money.

"There it is," he said. "One hundred and fifty thousand lire. You could get nothing good for less. Now we'll go to see Amleto."

He took Pierino along for company. Amleto lived in a wider street, in a ground-floor flat with a big yard at the back for his goods. He led them out through the kitchen to the yard, and there was the little Fiat under an open shed, away in at the back, covered with a sheet of plastic to keep the dust off.

"There she is," Amleto said, "waiting for you quietly all these months. Isn't she a beauty?"

She was a beauty indeed. The men lifted off the plastic and all three of them had a good look. She was grey, not very shiny but she would improve with polishing. Her chrome parts shone in fine style, and it had already been decided that Pierino would keep them so. In the back window, hanging from a thread, was a little stuffed figure of Garibaldi. There was no mistaking the hero, with his red shirt and long hair. He was holding a sword in his right hand.

"That's beautiful," Luca said. "Does he go with the car?"

"Yes, indeed. Garibaldi has been in this car from the beginning. My wife's mother made him. You have the saints on the front panel as well, of course, so you're guarded at both ends."

Amleto drove the car out of the yard, a slow business because it had to be taken carefully around the piles of goods into the street. Then he brought Pierino and Luca into the bar next door to drink a coffee.

"And I have a surprise for you," he said, handing Pierino a doughnut from the counter with the air of one who could have a doughnut whenever he felt like it. "I've paid the tax on her. Now don't thank me too much or I'll get no reward in heaven. It's not much and I like to help my friends."

"A good man, a fine man," Luca said when Amleto had gone. "If we had more like him in Rome, there would be a lot less misery. Now we'll take her home."

They drove slowly along the wide street and up towards Santa Maria in Transtevere, through smaller and smaller streets until they reached their own door and parked. Pierino's mother, Anna, and his small brother and sister, Tonino and Elena, all came out on the balcony and stood in a row to look.

"She's beautiful," they said. "Will there be room for us all?"

"Yes, there will," said Luca and they all came downstairs and tried it.

"We can go to Frascati to drink the wine and to Fregene to swim," Luca said, "but the most important thing is that we'll be able to bring the things to the market."

The market took place every Sunday. For three days before it, the flat was stuffed with all kinds of goods that could be sold there: fire-irons and metal dogs to lean them on, old pistols and swords, pictures in golden frames, usually chipped but sometimes in good order, folding stools and tables, book-ends in the shape of sea-horses or angels or pillars, lamps the same, boxes to keep anything and everything in, wire or wrought-iron baskets to hang pots of flowers in, books in strange languages as well as in Italian, sometimes with pictures, mirrors of all sizes with gold frames, sets of shelves to hang on the wall, vases and bowls for flowers, plates and dishes, glasses with coloured stems, statues of heroes of ancient Rome as well as statues of the Christian saints—one never knew what Luca would bring home. After he got the car he was able to buy much more. Each day he drove out to some little village to the south of Rome, coming back laden in the evening with all sorts of things, and also with baskets of all shapes and sizes.

"Now that I can carry them, I think I'll begin to specialise in baskets," he said. "I've been to Nemi and Grottaferrata, and I find that the people respect me now that I have my Five Hundred. They have the things ready waiting for me now, instead of hiding them from me to sell to someone who looks richer. It's a great thing to get known for something special—that's how you build up a battery of customers."

On Saturday evening, right after supper, everyone took a hand in loading the car. The china went in first, well packed around with old curtains and rugs. The baskets went on top, and some were tied on to the roof, so that the Five Hundred was a fine sight as she swayed down the lane to the street. There was room only for Luca inside but the rest of the family was quite content to walk. They had to cross the great avenue, Viale Trastevere, at the traffic lights to make sure of getting there alive, and then go down a winding street to where the market stretched from the old gate

called Porta Portese, almost to the railway
bridge.

By the time they got there, the big dealers
from Frosinone and Caserta and Naples had
arrived and were already setting up their fine
stalls and hanging up their goods, mostly new
clothes and curtains and bed-linen, from poles

at either end. They laid out tempting layers of shoes and toys and dungarees and underwear and aprons and dresses and furs, with the brightest colours on top to attract attention. Great coloured bedspreads hung like flags. Some stalls had home-made toffee with nuts in it, that would break your teeth if you were not careful. Some had ornaments and necklaces and earrings and brooches, glittering as darkness fell and the street lamps were lit.

All of these things were new but Pierino liked the old things better because you never knew what you would find among them.

Amleto laid out his furniture in the space next to theirs, big stuff, wardrobes and tables and armchairs, which fitted into his big van. He was shouting excitedly as he always did at this time, and his little round hat kept almost falling off his head as he jerked this way and that. Still he had time to call out to Luca:

"Ah, you capitalist! Now you're in a fine way of business!"

The people who had the stalls around heard him and came to admire the Five Hundred and congratulate Luca and wish him luck. Carmine and Alfredo, the two brothers who had the next stall at the other side, came over too.

"It's lovely," Carmine said enviously, stroking it. "I wish we had one like it."

"Grandeur!" said Alfredo. "Poor people shouldn't have big ideas."

There was no time then for anything but unloading the Five Hundred and laying out the goods as well as possible. Their space was not big—it was the same space that they had every week and that Luca's father had had before him—and they had to make sure that breakable things were kept to the back and small things that could be stolen were put all in one place where a sharp eye could be kept on them. That was Anna's job and nothing had ever been sneaked from under her eye. The baskets were ranged at one end, two or three of each kind grouped together. Now that summer had come, basket chairs would

1011.939/JFI

WESTMEATH COUNTY LIBRARY

be bought for the terraces. Luca had six ready, three big and three small.

As the evening went on, more and more stalls were set up and the market began to look very busy. Still no selling was allowed and the policemen strolled around to see that no one broke the rule. Raimondo, the fat, tired-looking one, stood for a long time by Luca's place, swinging his whistle on its cord. His white shoes and white suit were shining clean, a credit to his wife, Anna said, but Raimondo answered:

"The shoes, yes, but the suit goes to the laundry."

He took a step or two forward to see his watch properly in the light of the street lamp.

"Midnight," he said, and at that moment the clock on Santa Maria began to strike.

Raimondo waited respectfully until it had finished and then he blew a blast on his whistle. That was the signal that the selling could begin, the most exciting, marvellous moment of the whole week.

## 2

ALMOST immediately, it seemed, customers began to appear. The first to come were three tall, wide ladies with strong voices. Two of them had been to a party and they were telling the third about it as they fingered Luca's goods:

"It was a wretched party. I don't know why she gives these parties when she can't do it properly. Only soup and spaghetti and wine and little cakes—no champagne, no caviare savouries, and the olives not stuffed, and what can she expect? No one there, of course, but four cats."

"And yourselves," said the third lady, who had not been to the party.

Pierino's little sister Elena began to giggle and pull at Pierino so that he had to lean down to listen to her:

"Four cats at the party—and soup and spaghetti: I wish I had been there. Four cats!"

"She means there were only unimportant people there," Pierino explained but Elena went off giggling to tell her mother about it.

The wide ladies bought a gold plaster angel and a brass candlestick, turning them this way and that to see them in the lamplight. Luca said:

"They are not broken, ladies. When I say a thing is not broken, I tell the truth, not like some dealers who would cheat you at this time of the night when you can't see properly. But I know that if I please the customers they will come back again next week and the week after, for more. Now I'd like to show you my baskets—perhaps you need some new chairs for your terrace? If you buy mine here, you won't have to go out to the fairs in the country later on. These are the same baskets, I assure you."

"That would certainly save trouble and

money," said the wide ladies. "Every little counts, as we all know. Show us those chairs."

They bought two of them, but first all three of them had to sit in the chairs and try them for size and comfort, throwing themselves back in them and laying their arms along to see if they were the right height and length. When they had gone Luca said:

"Such nonsense! A chair is a chair. You'd think it was camels they were buying at the very least."

"Where are their husbands?" Anna asked without taking her eye off the part of the stall where the small things were now being fingered by other people.

"Gone, I suppose," said Luca. "I know I would, if I had a wife like that."

"Now, Luca! Don't speak like that in front of the children, if you please."

It was a fine night and for two or three hours people kept coming to the market, taking advantage of the coolness. By day it would be as hot as an oven. Most of the people were on their way home from visiting friends and needed a walk in the fresh air. At last there was no one. Pierino and Tonino and Elena lay down on a soft pile of old curtains for a sleep but Luca and Anna remained awake, resting their elbows on the stall sometimes and dozing a little but always springing to life again when there was the slightest movement near them. Some cats came slinking by—real cats, that lived in the ruined temple at Largo Argentina. They seemed to know when it was Saturday night, for they always crossed the river then and came for a jaunt to the market to see what they could pick up. People gave them ends of bread and sausage, which they had brought to eat during the long night and morning of the market, and as well as what they were given, they had their chances. In the early, early morning, Pierino saw three of them tussling over a whole roast chicken, having a glorious, appetite-raising fight and finishing up by dividing it almost equally between them.

The bars opened at six o'clock and Luca went off with Pierino to get coffee. When they would come back, Anna and Elena and Tonino could go. At the bar, Alfredo and Carmine were already sitting at one of the tables sipping their coffee. Luca said:

"Good morning. A fine day for work."

Alfredo answered politely enough but

Pierino noticed that Carmine almost growled at them. Luca went on:

"Did you do good business last night?"

"The usual," Alfredo said. "And you?"

"Better than usual," Luca said, "because I have more to sell. You should think of getting a Five Hundred too—it will pay for itself in time."

"Where would we get the money? They would take you by the throat these days, for a Five Hundred."

"Save up, as I did," Luca said eagerly. "It took a year but it's worth it."

Afterwards when they were standing at the counter drinking their coffee Pierino said:

"I don't think they liked your advice. They thought you were suggesting that they are extravagant."

"So they are," Luca said. "They had a good father, those boys, but they are too fond of comfort. Imagine paying extra to sit at a table outside when you could have your coffee at half the price standing at the counter!

That's how money is wasted. At this rate they'll never have the price of a Five Hundred."

Business was good that morning and by one o'clock when the market ended, Luca was feeling rich enough to say:

"Today we'll celebrate the Five Hundred by going to Frascati. We won't do this every

Sunday, mind! It would be madness to plan that. But just today we'll go, when we have brought all the things home."

They hurried over this and by five o'clock they were bowling along the ring road that goes all around Rome, with exits now and then to the little towns in the neighbourhood. Everyone else seemed to have had the same idea and at first the road was very crowded, but at last they were turning on to the Frascati road, past the restaurant called The Spit that had an eagle in a cage outside, then up and up among the olive trees, seeing Frascati clinging against the side of the hill like a painted picture, with the Villa Aldobrandini surrounded by trees in the exact middle of it. They drove slowly into the town, along by the side of the main square in front of the villa, through the narrow street into the square in front of the Cathedral, down another side street and out on to a great wide terrace that overlooked the valley. There the different wine shops had set out trestle tables with long benches at either side. The sun was very hot and the Five Hundred, packed with the whole family, had been like a little oven though no one liked to say so. For these good reasons they were all glad to find a table free in the shade. They sat on the benches and Anna

opened her bag of broad beans and spilled them out on the table while Pierino went to get a litre of wine. Then they stayed a long time in a half-dream, eating the beans, drinking the wine and looking at the beautiful landscape spread out below them, the grey-green olive trees in the fields and the brilliant blue wistaria that grew against the houses, and the red-tiled roofs and yellow walls of the villages that were scattered here and there in the valley.

When it was time to go home, Luca said:

"Perhaps we'll be able to come again, not every Sunday, of course, but now and then."

During the week it was good to be able to think sometimes of that wonderful day in Frascati. Pierino kept the Five Hundred shining clean, an oily rag on the chrome parts and a soft damp cloth on the glass. He found a piece of red thread and tied Garibaldi's shirt neatly in around his waist and straightened his sword.

On Saturday he helped as usual to load up

with the things for the market. This time there were some basket-work tables as well as chairs, which Luca had bought in Nemi, a celebrated place for basket-making. The tables were sold that very night, and Luca was looking pleased when they all settled down for a rest at three o'clock in the morning.

So a few weeks passed. One Sunday morning, after they had had their coffee, Luca said:

"I'd like a little mat of rubber, under my feet in the Five Hundred, when I go out into the country on those long drives. See if you can find me one at some motor-car stall."

He gave Pierino five hundred lire for the mat, which would be made to the exact size they needed. It was exciting to walk through the distant part of the market where the motor-car stalls were. There you could buy fenders and over-riders and door-locks and windscreen-wipers and lamps of all kinds, as well as mats and seat-covers and headrests and medals of the saints to protect your car from evil on the road. He found a stall that

specialised in things for Five Hundreds—
indeed it looked as if you could buy all the
pieces of a Five Hundred there and put one
together yourself, if you had the skill.

He picked out a green rubber mat, specially
for under the driver's feet. There was a little
pile of them there, and he found that he had
to go through them carefully to make sure of
finding a clean-looking, new one. While he
was doing this, the owner of the stall came
over to him and said:

"Friend, why don't you just take one?
You're mixing up all my mats. They're all the
same."

"Excuse me; they are not all the same,"
Pierino said politely. "Some are new and
some have been used, I think."

The man had pale-green eyes like a goat,
which he fixed on Pierino in a frightening way
as he said:

"You have a new mat in your hand. Take
it and be off with you."

Without a word, Pierino held out the five

coins. The man took them quickly and then
said in a sleepy drawl:

"Wait a moment. You're a smart boy. You
have your wits about you—isn't that so?"

"Yes, I suppose so."

"You know everyone in this market?"

"Not everyone. I know the people around my own part."

"Then you can do a little work for me and I'll pay you a hundred lire—no, two hundred lire every time. It's easy work—just keep your eyes open and your mouth shut and let me know if anyone buys a Five Hundred."

"Why?"

"So that I can sell them things for it, of course. That's my trade. Who is that mat for?"

"For my father. He has just bought one," Pierino said, swelling with pride at the memory of it.

"Wonderful. Who is your father?"

"Luca, with the stall beside Amleto the furniture dealer. My father can sell baskets now, since he has the Five Hundred."

"Very nice, very nice indeed."

But though the words were friendly, the goats' eyes were very cold, and as he went away Pierino knew that he would never work for that man, not at any price.

# 3

IT was three Sundays later that the Five Hundred disappeared. No one knew exactly when it was stolen—it seemed that one moment it was there and the next it was gone. Yet someone must have sneaked up at a busy time and pushed it away quietly. No one would have dared to start up the engine because the noise would have attracted attention but the little car was so small and light that it would have been quite easy to have opened the driver's door and with a hand on the wheel push it away into the crowd. Then in a free space it would have been started up and driven off. Everyone in Rome had a key to fit a Five Hundred so there was no difficulty there.

Pierino noticed that it was gone. He came running to Luca:

"Papa! Did you move our car?"

"No—of course not. Has someone asked us to move it?"

Luca hardly glanced around from the customer to whom he was selling a pair of iron fire-dogs. They were specially good ones, in the shape of dachshunds with brass toes, and the customer knew they were worth ten thousand lire but he wanted them for five. It was important business and still Pierino repeated:

"Papa! Our Five Hundred is gone!"

Holding an iron dog high, Luca said:

"Gone?"

He put the fire-dog down slowly and gazed at the space where the car had been. Then, half to himself, he said:

"It's gone, sure enough. Where?" Suddenly he was shouting: "Where—where—where is my new Five Hundred that I saved for during a whole year? What lazy, idle son of an idle father has stolen my little car? When I find him—"

Anna came scuttling over to say:
"Luca! The children! Mind what you say!
What has happened? Why are you shouting?"

"My new Five Hundred is gone!"

"Perhaps you didn't put it in the usual place today. How can it be gone?"

"Yes, I put it in the usual place," Luca said, lowering his voice somewhat, "and it can be gone because Rome is full of thieves and robbers that would take the milk out of a poor man's coffee and come back for the sugar. By Bacchus, when I find that—"

"Language, language!" said Anna. "That sort of talk never solved anything. We must call the police."

"There's a policeman here," said Pierino, and sure enough, a short, fat policeman, not their usual Raimondo, was coming towards them, having heard Luca's shouts.

"What's all this about?" he asked sharply. "Who is creating the noise and disturbance?"

He looked angrily from one to another of them and Luca said indignantly:

"I'm making the noise and I'm shouting, and so would you if your new Five Hundred were stolen right from under your nose while

41

you were quietly getting on with your business—"

"A new Five Hundred? What colour was it? What was its number? When did you miss it? When did you see it last? Where was it parked?"

"Give me a chance," said poor Luca, his head spinning with all the questions. "It's not a new Five Hundred—I bought it second-hand, from Amleto—"

"You said a moment ago that it was a new Five Hundred."

"I meant new to me, of course. Its number is Roma 772725."

"That's quite an old Five Hundred, then. With that number, it must have been registered in 1965 at least."

"I suppose so but I don't care what age it is. I want it back. It's grey, and my son missed it a few minutes ago. It was parked right over there, where I always park it."

"I'll give you seven thousand for the fire-dogs," the customer interrupted.

"I won't sell under ten," Luca said. "I'm surrounded by robbers, one taking away my Five Hundred that I love like my life, and now another wanting to take away my little dogs with the brass toes for a mean seven thousand lire, when all Rome knows that they're worth ten at the least." He glared at the customer, a thin anxious man with a black hat and a fine silk scarf. "Friend, what is your trade?"

"I'm a musician," said the customer, looking frightened.

"And when you play your music, do people try to make you do it for a small price? Do they say: 'Two tunes for the price of one'? Or do they say: 'This is an artist—let us pay him his price'?"

"I'll give you ten thousand," the customer said hurriedly and he threw a note on the stall and seized the dogs, one under each arm, and walked away.

"That's something, at least," said Luca, putting away the note in his wallet. He turned to the policeman. "Have you not yet started to find my Five Hundred? Is it for this we pay taxes? At once, at once! It must be found."

"Easy, easy," said the policeman. "Now just give me all the details again, if you please."

He got out his book and a pen and made Luca tell him slowly, several times over, what he had told him already: the number of the car, where it had been parked, where he usually left it, when he had last seen it, who had missed it. Pierino was watching silently and it seemed to him that the policeman was being very stupid, delaying too long and asking questions to which he had already had the answers. It was a rather simple matter, after all, since as Luca had said, Five Hundreds were stolen in Rome almost every day of the week. Carmine and Alfredo had joined in the conversation now, and were suggesting that Luca had perhaps been mistaken about the time when the car was stolen.

"I think it was stolen while you were asleep,"

Alfredo said but Luca said indignantly:

"I didn't sleep at all, and besides I remember seeing the car just before that man came to buy the fire-dogs with the brass toes."

"We'll ask that boy that noticed the Five Hundred was gone," the policeman said, turning around to look for Pierino.

But Pierino had ducked low out of sight and was hiding under the stall. He heard all the voices call:

"Pierino! Where are you? Come and tell the policeman about the Five Hundred! Where is that boy? He was here a moment ago. Pierino!"

Pierino stayed very quiet until at last he heard the policeman say:

"It's no use waiting any longer. Better for me to go and begin my enquiries. After all, you have told me everything the boy knows."

Luca said, sounding very dejected:

"Yes, that is best. Do go and try to find my car. My whole business, my whole life depends on it."

Anna said consolingly:

"Don't sound so sad. We managed all right before we had the Five Hundred. We'll get along all right without it now. And perhaps it will be found soon."

"I'm afraid it will never be found," Luca said sadly. "When a Five Hundred disappears like that, usually it is never seen again."

These were terrible words. Pierino felt himself weighed down with them, almost as if it were not worth while trying to discover what had happened to the car. It was his father's weary, sad voice that decided him to try. It seemed so unjust and unfair that such a good, honest man should have his hard work gone for nothing.

Pierino sneaked out from under the stall and followed the cross policeman, keeping well down out of sight and ready to duck in under a hanging curtain, or another stall, or into the crowd, if the man were to turn. Pierino knew him by a streak of greenish paint on the leg of his uniform, paint that had dried in and could not be removed by the laundry. The trousers looked more worn than the rest of the suit. Indeed it was not like a real policeman's suit at all. Sometimes the policeman stopped for a minute or two and stood by a stall listening to the conversation of the owners and the customers but whenever he did this, all talk soon died away and

the people got very busy at something else than chat. Most of the time he walked slowly, a more sensible plan Pierino thought, because then he seemed always to be either just coming or just going, never actually stopped to listen. Now and then he paused at a sweet stall and took one or two sweets to eat but he never offered to pay for them, and though the owners saw him they never asked him for the money. He certainly was a strange policeman, and Pierino was glad he had had the sense to follow him.

They went past the clothes and furniture stalls, past the sweet stalls, past the fortune-tellers whose birds would pick out your fortune for ten lire, past the shoe stalls and then they were in the section of the market where parts of cars were sold. Perhaps this policeman was not such a fool, after all, Pierino said to himself. He rambled along, sometimes greeting a stall-holder he knew or looking over the stalls that sold mascots for cars. Once he had a coffee at a bar, standing sideways with the cup in his hand and watching the people pass by. When he had finished, he laid down his cup and said to the barman:

"Thank you, and good day to you."

He stood for a moment and then strolled on, through the double line of stalls, looking casually at the things that were displayed, until he was exactly opposite the stall where Pierino had bought the mat three weeks ago. Fearing that the goat-eyed man would recognise him, Pierino slipped around to the back of the stall where there was just space enough for him to pass. All around him, voices twittered and chattered as people discussed the value and price of the things that were for sale. Then he heard two voices he recognised, having a soft conversation. One was the policeman—there was no mistaking that voice, which had been so sharp with Luca a short time ago, now cooing like a dove for quietness. The other was the voice of the man with eyes like a goat, a hissing voice like the voice of a snake, saying softly:

"Well, friend, is all well at the other end of the market?"

"All is well," said the policeman. "An honest, simple man, just like his son, no danger to anyone. He has left the whole problem to me. We can take it away to the cave quite safely—the sooner the better."

Then they both laughed quietly, with a sound like bubbles in a vat of witch's poison, and the policeman strolled on.

# 4

FOR a full minute Pierino could not move from his hiding-place behind the stall. He was shocked through and through to think that a policeman could be dishonest. Who could be trusted, if you could not trust the police? What would become of poor Luca, who had saved every lira of the price of the Five Hundred with such trouble? Worst of all, he could see that he had directed the thieves to the Five Hundred himself, by his boasting talk. Pierino could hardly bear it. He began to make his way back to his father's stall, try-ing to think of someone, any single person who could help him. He could ask Amleto, perhaps, but who could say that even Amleto could be trusted? And there was Raimondo —but perhaps he was a friend of the short, fat policeman and would be furious with

Pierino for saying a word against him. Even Raimondo himself could be a thief.

But Pierino could not believe this of Raimondo, whom he had known all his life. Back at the stall, there he was and Luca was telling him that the Five Hundred was gone and that the short, fat policeman had written down all the details about it.

"But if he were to write a book as long as the Holy Bible about it, he won't get back my Five Hundred," said poor Luca.

"Did he say he would start enquiries?"

"That's exactly what he said. He went off to do something about it, though he didn't say what."

"He can do all sorts of things. I'm sorry I was not here myself, but I was called away to the other side of the street just then—I was told there had been a robbery there but when I got there, though I asked everyone, no one seemed to know anything about it."

Pierino asked Raimondo:

"What becomes of cars that are stolen like

that? I'd know our Five Hundred anywhere in Rome. Will they bring it to another part of Italy to sell it?"

"No, they have a much easier way," Raimondo said. "The car thieves have special places where they keep the cars, especially the Five Hundreds which are so much alike and so plentiful, and they just take them apart. Then they build up new cars out of the pieces, so that the doors of your Five Hundred and the tyres of another and the wings of another and the windscreen of another and the bumpers of another would all be together in a completely new car. In this way they make sure that no one can possibly recognise his own car again."

"In that case it seems that the most important thing is to find our Five Hundred quickly, before they have time to take it to the factory."

"Quite right," said Raimondo. "I must find that policeman you spoke to. Short and fat, you said."

"Yes, with very black hair and eyebrows and a smile like a cat—"

"Did you notice his number?"

"No."

"That's a pity—it would be the easiest way to find him. Just go off through the market now and see if you can find him. He can't be far off. Fetch him here." Raimondo frowned. "I can't remember a short, fat policeman with a smile like a cat."

Pierino left Raimondo and Luca with their heads together, he was quite sure that he did not want to deliver that message to the strange policeman. Still he began to wander through the market, pausing every time he saw a white helmet sticking up above the heads of the crowd. He saw policemen of all shapes and sizes and ages but no sign of the cat-faced one. Minute by minute the morning was passing away. Soon the market would be over and then there would be no hope at all of finding the Five Hundred.

In despair he moved gradually towards the

stall of the goat-eyed man. He found him selling a pair of over-riders to a small, weedy man who was carrying a baby under one arm. Pierino heard him say:

"These are fine ones, not quite new but who can afford to have new things? These were taken off a car that was about to die and would not need them any more. You can have them at half the price you would pay for new ones."

Keeping out of the man's sight, Pierino edged around behind the stall as he had done before. Suddenly he stopped dead and felt his head swim for one awful second. There, stuffed in at the back of the stall with some other mascots for cars, was the Five Hundred's Garibaldi. There could be no mistake about it. Pierino did not dare to reach out a hand and take it but he could see that it was his by the thread that tied the hero's shirt in neatly around his waist.

The man with the baby was going off with the over-riders under his other arm, and the

goat-eyed man might turn at any moment. Pierino dodged in behind the stall, out of breath as if he had been running. Now that he had the evidence, should he go back at once and fetch Raimondo and have the goat-eyed man arrested? This might not be so easy. It was Sunday and Raimondo would need a warrant or at least some authority from his superiors before he could arrest anyone. There would be a long delay, during which the Five Hundred could be driven away to that abominable factory and taken to pieces by those cannibals.

A cave, the policeman had said to the goat-eyed man. Pierino had forgotten that part until now. There could not be a cave in Rome, surely, but perhaps it was some sort of a slang name for the factory.

Moving along behind the stall, Pierino saw at his feet a small white bundle. It was rolled up carelessly, as if it had been done in a hurry. He pushed at it with his foot and opened it out. What he saw was hardly a surprise now:

a white jacket with black épaulettes, a white policeman's helmet and a pair of white trousers with a stain of green paint on one leg.

Like a fish he slipped out into the crowd and away towards Luca's stall. He had to move slowly because a running boy would be sure to attract attention, but he felt safer when he was in his own part of the market.

At the stall he found that Raimondo was not there but Carmine and Alfredo were talking excitedly to Luca. Carmine said:

"Those thieves were very bold—they must be clever ones. To have the nerve to come right up and take the Five Hundred away, when you might have turned at any moment and seen it! That takes courage."

Alfredo said:

"It's hardly worth while trying to catch clever thieves like those. You would do better to forget you ever had a Five Hundred. After all, you did without a car for so many years, you can do without it now."

"That's what I've been telling him," Anna said, "but he won't believe me. He just keeps on saying that we did twice the business since we have had the car."

"And besides," Alfredo said, "the thieves would revenge themselves on you if they were caught. It would hardly be worth risking that."

"An honest man is not afraid of thieves," said Luca, "and the thieves would be in gaol

if they were caught, and could not harm anyone. It's my duty to have them caught if I
can, because you may be sure they have not
stolen only my Five Hundred."

Alfredo's eyes flashed with anger but he
could say no more. He turned back to his
stall and began to rearrange his things while
Carmine said in a strangely smooth tone:

"Life goes like that, friend—up and down,
and never the same for long."

Then Alfredo called him away sharply. It
was not hard to see that they were pleased at
the loss of the Five Hundred, and not hard to
understand why. Since he had had it, Luca's
stand was so full of enticing things that the
customers had only a glance in passing for
Alfredo's. Now they would be equal again.

Raimondo was coming towards them, push-
ing his way through the crowd, looking hot
and angry.

"Such a day!" he said. "Nothing goes
right. I've just been over again looking for
those people that were supposed to have been

robbed and still no one knows who they are or what they were robbed of. I'm sick and tired of asking foolish questions. At last I said to them: 'If you don't know which of you was robbed and of what, how can I do anything about it.' Did you find that policeman?"

"No," Pierino said. "Who sent you to look for some people that had been robbed in the first place?"

"I went in such a hurry that I can hardly remember," Raimondo said. "I was here, and a man came rushing up—yes, it was your neighbour, Alfredo, very excited, shouting: 'Quick, over to the far side—Silvio's stall has been robbed—next to the toffee stall, beside the one that sells pickled pigs' ears with lemon—' He gave a lot of details like that, so I took it that he knew exactly what had happened." Raimondo stopped suddenly and it was as if a light had been turned on inside his head. "Alfredo! He knew a lot about it then—he can answer some questions now."

## 5

RAIMONDO walked straight over to Alfredo and said:

"Who told you that there had been a robbery at the other side of the street?"

"I don't know—a man came by and said it—" Alfredo stammered.

"You said it was at Silvio's stall, beside the one that sells pickled pigs' ears with lemon —did the man tell you all that in one word?"

"Are you blaming me?" Alfredo shouted. "Do you think I shouldn't have told you about that robbery?"

"There was no robbery," Raimondo said. "No one over there has heard of a robbery and Silvio has all his property safe and sound. You wanted me out of the way."

"Why should I want you out of the way?"

Alfredo said reasonably. "It's nothing to me where you go in this market, so long as you're doing your duty."

Suddenly Carmine began to scream at Alfredo:

"You see, you're too clever for your own good—I always told you so and Mother said the same—don't deny you often heard it and it's your ruin now, yes, and mine too. I said it would be found out sooner or later—"

Alfredo sat down on the box that he always used as a seat beside his stall and put his head in his hands. Luca and Raimondo looked at each other in amazement, unable to speak. Pierino stayed perfectly still too, though now he guessed what had happened. Then Alfredo raised his head and looked at his brother with a tired expression, saying:

"Mother never said *you* were too clever for your good, or anyone else's. You could ruin a whole family without help from anyone."

Raimondo raised his shoulders and spread his hands in a helpless way, looking down at

Alfredo whose head was down in his hands again. Then Luca said gently:

"Alfredino, we all make mistakes. Tell me at least what happened and we'll see if it can't be put right. No one wants to ruin you. We're all neighbours and we only want to help you if we can."

Alfredo did not look up for a moment or two. Then suddenly he said to Luca:

"*I* wanted to ruin *you*—that's why I diverted Raimondo when the man came to push away your Five Hundred. Oh, I didn't do it on the spur of the moment. He came every Saturday night for three weeks to suggest it, and the third Saturday he persuaded me to do it. He had noticed that Raimondo is a friend of yours and stands near your stall a lot, and of course this is his special part of the market. So he knew it would not be easy to push away the Five Hundred unless Raimondo could be sent off somewhere else at the right moment."

"What did this man look like?" Pierino

asked. "Was he short and fat, with a face like a cat?"

"No," Alfredo said in surprise. "He was tall and thin—"

"With yellow eyes like a goat?" Pierino asked softly.

"Yes, now that you mention it. He had strange yellow eyes. Do you know him?"

"Yes." And he told how he had seen the little Garibaldi on the stall, with his shirt tied into his waist with a piece of red thread. "And I looked all around that part of the market but our Five Hundred is not there. And another thing—the man who was dressed as a policeman is not a policeman at all. I found his white suit in a bundle under the stall, the helmet too. I knew the clothes by the streak of green paint on the trousers. How could he have got them?"

"He must have stolen them. Perhaps the trousers belonged to a painter—no Roman policeman would have a streak of green paint on his uniform. Now the question is to find that Five Hundred before they take it to pieces. How can that be done, when there are almost as many Five Hundreds as Romans?"

"They mentioned a cave," Pierino said.

"And they mentioned Albano," said Alfredo, "or a place near Albano—with a strange name—Pavone—I can't remember—"

"There is a village called Pavona," Raimondo said. "I have an aunt who lives in Albano and that's how I know the district. It's on the way to the sea, Pavona. To work!" He looked around sharply. "Luca, you come with me, and we'll take the boy who knows the man with eyes like a goat. Signora," he said to Anna, "you can stay and mind the stall. I'll send my brother to help you to bring the things home when the market closes. Alfredo and Carmine will help too."

"Yes, yes," they said eagerly.

"That takes care of everything," Raimondo said. "Off we go, at once!"

"But is it dangerous?" Anna asked trembling.

"Even daily life is dangerous," Raimondo said, "but you needn't worry—we'll call at the station for reinforcements and a fine big car that will hold us all."

At the station he explained to the sergeant that the search had been delayed by a short, fat man pretending to be a policeman, smiling like a cat and behaving like a thief. All the policemen got very angry when they heard this.

"How can we expect the people to love us?" they said. "There's our notice up on the wall: 'In a free country, the police are at the service of the people.' Who is going to believe we're at their service when men dressed like policemen go about deceiving people like this?"

"I suppose it doesn't happen often," Pierino said.

"It happens more often than we like," they said.

Raimondo telephoned his brother, who was resting at home after a hard week's work in the General Post Office. Some outdoor

exercise would be good for him, Raimondo
said, and there would be the satisfaction of
helping a woman in distress. In the meantime
the sergeant was getting out the station car, a
big one with extra seats which they filled up

with policemen, all in plain clothes. No sooner were the doors closed than the driver curved out into the traffic which was running three deep along beside the river. People were already on their way to the sea, he said, but as it was near lunch-time some were sure to turn off and visit their mother-in-law on the way. Sure enough, as they went along the crowd thinned out and soon they were on the ring road, on their way to Albano. Alert as dogs, the policemen sat straight and tense in the car, paying special heed to every Five Hundred they saw even if it was clear that it was only a quiet family going to the sea. Every now and then one of them would say to Pierino:

"Roma 772725 is the number, you said?"

Or perhaps:

"Yellow eyes like a goat, you said?"

Or:

"A round smiling face like a cat, you said?"

Pierino said to everything:

"That's right. It won't be hard to know them, if we see them."

Soon they were climbing up to Frascati, skirting it and taking the Albano road, by long avenues of trees through Castelgandolfo, past the lake that lay as still as a bowl of cream, until they came to Albano itself, high on its own hill.

"Pavona is down there," Raimondo said, pointing. A long straggling road, bordered by pines, led down towards the distant sea. "We could go down there at once but it might be well to call on my Aunt Maria first. She's not a policeman's aunt for nothing."

She had a tiny pizzaria in a narrow street, five tables and an oven in the corner to make the pizzas, which were flat pies of pasta covered with tomato sauce and garlic. When the weather was hot, as it was now, she just put the tables outside on the pavement. Five families were sitting there, as it was already time to eat, with five litres of wine in front of them, and the glorious aroma of the hot tomatoes and garlic filled the air for yards around. They all went into the restaurant which was bare except for one big table. It was dark in there, but very hot because of the open-fronted oven in the corner. Raimondo's aunt whirled around from it and said:

"Welcome, every one of you. I hope you're not too hungry because there won't be a table free for nearly an hour—"

"It's all right, Zia Maria," Raimondo said. "We can't afford to stop."

"You're at work," she said alertly, her eyes lighting up with excitement.

"Looking for a cave full of cars, which we think is somewhere near Pavona," Raimondo said in a low voice. "Have you heard of anything?"

"Not directly," she said, "but last week someone said it's a very funny thing that Annibale who has the garage in Pavona should be able to buy himself a new Alfa Romeo, though the whole world knows that no one lives in Pavona and there are two garages there and hardly enough business for one. And his wife, Paola, had three new dresses already this year. *Mamma mia!* The pizza is burning!" She seized the long-handled shovel on which the pizza sat and snatched it out of the oven. "You go down to

76

Pavona and go through Annibale's garage. That's the best advice I can give you. Come back later and tell me how you fared, and eat a pizza of course."

They came out very quietly, because of the eating customers at the tables, but when they were safely in the car again Luca said:

"That's a useful aunt for a policeman, Raimondo."

"She knows everything that happens for miles around," Raimondo said. "She's not so useful to me because I'm stationed in Rome but if ever I have business out in the Castelli, she knows every inch of the ground. Funny thing, she hardly ever stirs outside her pizzaria. The news comes in to her."

They drove down the road towards Pavona and now Pierino began to feel a sort of fluttering inside him at what was to come. The size of the policemen was a comfort, though of course he hoped it would not come to a fight. The whirling, downhill road seemed to swallow them up so that they were at the cross-roads of Pavona much too soon.

They turned off to the right along a nar-
rower road and came to the village, set among
little hills. It was hardly a village—just a bar
and a little fly-blown shop and the two

garages that Zia Maria had mentioned. A young man in dark-blue trousers and a pale-blue shirt was standing outside one of the garages, dusting a new Alfa Romeo with a green and pink woolly duster on a stick. The driver said:

"Sit back, boys, and relax."

He turned in to the garage and stopped at the pump. The men leaned back against the seats and smiled gently but to Pierino they still looked just like five policemen. It must have been so too with the man in the pale-blue shirt. He bent his neck to look inside the car and then without a word he turned and scuttled into the garage.

With one look at each other, not smiling now, the policemen opened the doors and galloped after him, preventing him just in time from closing the doors against them. More slowly, Pierino and Luca got out and stood together in the hot sun. Even the driver was gone. Luca said:

"Listen!"

"I hear shouts and trampling. We'd be better off inside. If they come running out, I'd rather not be in their way."

"Into the garage, then."

Cautiously they went into the little building. It was set close against the hill, with double doors just wide enough to let a car through. One or two dusty old cars were pushed away at either side and a new placard advertising Pirelli tyres shone from one wall, but still the garage had an unused look.

At once they saw a small door, which might have been the door of a store-room, standing open now on to a dark passage beyond the garage. The shouts came from there. Close together, they went through to the passage-way and followed it for several yards, until it opened out into the cave. Then they stood still and gazed around in amazement.

It was a pear-shaped cave with the narrow end backing onto the garage. Electric bulbs on a loose wire hung from the ceiling and a powerful electric motor was set up in one corner. Beside it was a rack with tools for welding and cutting metal, as well as all the usual garage tools. At one side of this rack a huge collection of parts of cars was piled up neatly—doors, wings, fenders, windshields,

roofs and wheels—and at the other side there was a half-assembled Fiat Six Hundred on which the thieves had been working when the police broke in.

At the farthest end, next to another pair of

open doors which led out of the cave into the open country, Pierino saw their own Five Hundred. It was just as they had seen it last, not a door nor a wheel missing. They had arrived in time.

The goat-eyed man and the cat-faced man were each held in the grip of two policemen, and still Pierino shivered when he saw them. One policeman held the man who had been outside, still carrying his woolly duster on its stick. Tools spread in disorder on the floor and the swinging back doors showed that some others must have got away. The goat-eyed man said:

"Rats! They run at the first sign of danger."

And the cat-faced man said softly:

"After all, that is reasonable. In their position we would do the same."

The driver of the police car led the way outside and Raimondo said:

"There won't be room for you now in the police car but after all you have your Five Hundred. You can go in that and I'll come

with you, if I may. I'd prefer your company—besides we must go back to Zia Maria and tell her all about it, and eat a pizza as she said."

"What will happen to all those other cars?"

Raimondo lifted his shoulders and spread his hands.

"This place will be locked up and they will try to find the owners. Who knows what may be possible?"

"I am so sorry for their owners," Luca said as he climbed into the Five Hundred and drove it outside. Raimondo and Pierino followed, into a narrow lane overgrown with bushes which concealed the doors that had been let into the opening of the cave. The Five Hundred brushed the heavy leaves aside in its passage. They drove along the lane, out on to the main road, and found themselves to the west of the garage. As they passed it by, on their way back to Albano, they saw that its doors had been shut tightly and a huge padlock had been put on.

With no other customers to attend to, Maria was able to sit with them and hear the whole story, first from Raimondo, then from Luca and lastly from Pierino.

"It ended well," she said. "And I'll make you a new Garibaldi in case yours doesn't come back."

"What if he does come back?"

"Perhaps it would be better to make you Mrs. Garibaldi then—if he comes back, she can always hang beside him."

# Also by Eilís Dillon

### THE LOST ISLAND

The lost island is a mystery. No one knows where it is – or whether it even exists. But everyone knows that some great reward is to be found there by any-one brave enough to seek it. Michael's father set out to find the lost island, but never returned. Now it is Michael's turn. He gets a boat and with his friend, Joe, sets off across unknown seas to try to discover the island's secret.

Paperback £3.95/€5.07/$7.95

### THE HOUSE ON THE SHORE

Jim O'Malley has never met his wealthy Uncle Martin from Cloghan-more, so when he is sent to live with him he is not sure what to expect. But nothing could prepare him for what happens next. He finds a village torn by rumour and revenge. His uncle has disappeared and his house is lying empty. When Jim investigates he is threatened by two ruthless strangers. Just what are they after? And can Jim uncover the truth about his uncle before it's too late?

Paperback £4.99/€6.34/$7.95

## LIVING IN IMPERIAL ROME

A vivid reconstruction, in words and pictures, of life under Trajan the Emperor, nearly 2000 years ago. Four different families brought to life, set with historical accuracy in the drama of imperial Rome. Tourists can still visit these historic streets and buildings. For young or old, student or tourist, this is a living history of an important and vibrant city.

Paperback £4.95/€6.34/$7.95

## THE LUCKY BAG

*Eds. Eilís Dillon, Pat Donlon, Patricia Egan, Peter Fallon*
*Illustrated by Martin Gale*

This collection includes folk tales, fairy tales, and more modern stories of adventure, excitement and growing up. It contains work from our best-loved writers – Jonathan Swift, Frank O'Connor, Seán O'Faoláin, Brian Friel, Mary Lavin – as well as discoveries from little-known authors and specially commissioned translations from Irish language classics.

Paperback £4.95/€6.34/$7.95

# OTHER BOOKS FROM THE O'BRIEN PRESS

**ENCHANTED JOURNEYS: Fifty Years of Irish Writing for Children**
*Ed. Robert Dunbar*
*Illustrated by Aileen Johnston*

The very best of recent Irish writing for children, selected by an expert in children's literature. Extracts from: Eilís Dillon, Marita Conlon-McKenna, Frank Murphy, Maeve Friel, Tom McCaughren, Elizabeth O'Hara, Sam McBratney, Siobhán Parkinson, Matthew Sweeney, Martin Waddell, John Quinn, Eugene McCabe, Janet McNeill, Meta Mayne Reid, Walter Macken, Patricia Lynch and Conor O'Brien.

Hardback £8.99/€11.41/$14.95

**SECRET LANDS: The World of Patricia Lynch**
*Ed. Robert Dunbar*
*Illustrated by Aileen Johnston*

An anthology of the work of one of Ireland's best-loved authors: Patricia Lynch. These stories explore a magical world of strange and wonderful characters, including the infamous Brogeen the leprechaun, but they also provide a touching insight into Irish society from the 1930s to 1960s.

Hardback £8.99/€11.41/$14.95

### THE KING'S SECRET

*Patricia Forde*
*Illustrated by Donald Teskey*

A wacky retelling of the classic 'hairy story' about the BIG secret of King Lowry Lynch. No one must cut his hair, for if they do they will die!

Paperback £3.99/€5.07/$7.95

### ART, YOU'RE MAGIC!

*Sam McBratney*
*Illustrated by Tony Blundell*

When Mervyn Magee comes to school sporting a new blue tie, Art wants one just like it. When Mum buys him a butterfly tie, he feels sure that now his classmates will like him better. But his beautiful new tie proves to be nothing but trouble!

Paperback £3.50/€5.07

### THE LEPRECHAUN WHO WISHED HE WASN'T

*Siobhán Parkinson/Illus. Donald Teskey*

Laurence is a leprechaun. He has been small for 1,100 years and *hates* it! He wants to be TALL! Then he meets Phoebe, a large girl who wants to be small. She invites him to live in her house and Laurence is delighted. But there is one thing about leprechauns that you can't change – they are always up to mischief!

Paperback £3.99/€5.07/$6.95

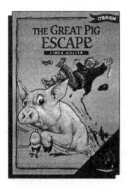

### THE GREAT PIG ESCAPE
*Linda Moller*

The farm cat, Runtling, warns the pigs of what lies in store for them at the market. Together the thirteen pigs escape and make their way across country, learning all sorts of things about themselves, about humans and about the world outside the farmyard. But it's not easy to find a safe place to live ...

Price £4.99/€6.34/$7.95

### JIMEEN
*Pádraig Ó Siochfhradha*

Jimeen can't seem to stay out of trouble – whether it's tormenting his sister, Cáit, a night out 'on the Wren', trying to steal lobsters, or scouring the countryside for spies. Popular for years in the Irish language, this translation means that a whole new audience can join in the fun.

Price £4.99/€6.34/$7.95

### CHARLIE HARTE AND HIS TWO-WHEELED TIGER
*Frank Murphy*

Charlie wants a bike, but his family cannot afford one. So he assembles his own strange-looking machine from old bits and pieces. But when his bike seems to develop a life of its own, Charlie's life is changed forever ...

Price £3.99/€5.07/$7.95